PUFFIN BO

The Day We Brightened
Up the School

Other titles in the First Young Puffin series

BEAR'S BAD MOOD John Prater
BELLA AT THE BALLET Brian Ball
BLESSU Dick King-Smith
BUBBLEGUM BOTHER Wendy Smith
DAD, ME AND THE DINOSAURS Jenny Koralek
THE DAY THE SMELLS WENT WRONG Catherine Sefton
HARRY'S AUNT Sheila Lavelle
DIZ AND THE BIG FAT BURGLAR Margaret Stuart Barry
DUMPLING Dick King-Smith
ERIC'S ELEPHANT GOES CAMPING John Gatehouse
ERIC'S ELEPHANT ON HOLIDAY John Gatehouse
FETCH THE SLIPPER Sheila Lavelle
GERALDINE GETS LUCKY Robert Leeson
GOODNIGHT, MONSTER Carolyn Dinan
HAPPY CHRISTMAS, RITA! Hilda Offen
HARRY'S AUNT Sheila Lavelle
HOP IT, DUGGY DOG! Brian Ball
THE INCREDIBLE SHRINKING HIPPO Stephanie Baudet
THE JEALOUS GIANT Kaye Umansky
NINA THE GOBBLEDEGOAT Penny Ives
PINK FOR POLAR BEAR Valerie Solís
THE POCKET ELEPHANT Catherine Sefton
THE QUEEN'S BIRTHDAY HAT Margaret Ryan
RAJ IN CHARGE Andrew and Diana Davies
RITA IN WONDERWORLD Hilda Offen
RITA THE RESCUER Hilda Offen
ROLL UP! ROLL UP! IT'S RITA Hilda Offen
THE ROMANTIC GIANT Kaye Umansky
SOS FOR RITA Hilda Offen
SPACE DOG SHOCK Andrew and Paula Martyr
THANK YOU DUGGY DOG Brian Ball and Lesley Smith
WHAT STELLA SAW Wendy Smith
WOOLLY JUMPERS Peta Blackwell

The Day We Brightened Up the School

Mick Gowar

Illustrated by
Paula Martyr

PUFFIN BOOKS

PUFFIN BOOKS

Published by the Penguin Group
Penguin Books Ltd, 80 Strand, London WC2R 0RL, England
Penguin Putnam Inc., 375 Hudson Street, New York, New York 10014, USA
Penguin Books Australia Ltd, 250 Camberwell Road, Camberwell, Victoria 3124, Australia
Penguin Books Canada Ltd, 10 Alcorn Avenue, Toronto, Ontario, Canada M4V 3B2
Penguin Books India (P) Ltd, 11 Community Centre, Panchsheel Park, New Delhi – 110 017, India
Penguin Books (NZ) Ltd, Cnr Rosedale and Airborne Roads, Albany, Auckland, New Zealand
Penguin Books (South Africa) (Pty) Ltd, 24 Sturdee Avenue, Rosebank 2196, South Africa

Penguin Books Ltd, Registered Offices: 80 Strand, London WC2R 0RL, England

www.penguin.com

First published by Hamish Hamilton Ltd 1995
Published in Puffin Books 1997
7 9 10 8

Text copyright © Mick Gower, 1995
Illustrations copyright © Paula Martyr, 1995
All rights reserved

The moral right of the author and illustrator has been asserted

Printed and bound in China by Leo Paper Products Ltd

0–140–38613–0

"This week is going to be a *special* week," said Mrs Thompson, our Head Teacher, at the end of Assembly. "This week we're going to brighten up the school.

"Class One are going to paint Spring pictures to decorate the corridors.

Class Two are going to write Spring poems to pin up in the Entrance Hall.

And Class Three are going to paint a mural on the playground wall."

Miss Bennett, our teacher, told us what a
mural was.

"A giant picture painted on to a
wall . . ."

7

Everyone had good ideas.

"Let's do a space picture, with rockets, flying saucers, exploding suns and shooting stars," said Jason.

"That's boring!" groaned Kylie. "Let's do a sea picture, with waves on top, and underneath the water – fish and eels and a big sea creature like the Loch Ness Monster!"

"That's no good!" sneered Keith. "Let's do a war picture with guns and tanks and fighter planes – "

"No, no!" yelled everybody else.

"Cowboys and Indians – "

"A pirate ship – "
"Sleeping Beauty's castle – "
"Snow White and the Seven Dwarfs – "
"Dracula – "

"STOP!" yelled Miss Bennett. "*Spring* is
the topic for the week – so it will be a
Spring picture with daffodils and crocuses
and baby lambs. Put on your painting
clothes, this could be rather messy."

Miss divided us into groups.

"Has everyone got paint and brushes?"

"Yes, Miss."

"Group One will do the sky. Group Two will do the grass."

We started. It took *hours* to paint a tiny
bit of sky, a tiny bit of grass.

"I've got a good idea," said Jason. "It'd
be much quicker if we slosh the paint
straight out of the tin – like this!"

"STOP!" yelled Miss Bennett.

Too late!

"Ooooh, Miss!" cried Sasha. "Mark's got blue hair . . . so's Jon and Melanie."

"Look at my trousers, Miss," said Tom. "My mum'll *kill* me!"

"Tom, come with me. The rest of you wait here," said Miss Bennett. "And no more throwing paint."

We watched the giant swirl of paint drip down the wall.

"It looks just like a wave," said Kylie. And she got a brush and started painting fish.

"Ummmm! I'm telling Miss," said Sasha. "Fish aren't allowed. It's got to be a Spring picture, Miss said."

"MIND YOUR OWN BUSINESS!"
yelled Kylie.

"Miss, Miss – " said Sasha. "Look
what – "

Kylie raised her brush.

"STOP!" yelled Miss Bennett from across the playground.

Too late!

Splat! went the paint.

"Owwww!" wailed Sasha. "I've got paint in my eyes and it hurts!"

"Kylie, go to Mrs Thompson!" snapped
Miss Bennett. "Sasha, come with me. The
rest of you, start painting daffodils and
crocuses. And no more paint fights!"

We started painting crocuses. It took
hours.

"I've got a good idea," said Lee.
"Instead of painting flowers we could *print*
them with our hands. Like finger-painting –
only bigger."

21

Lee dipped his hands into the paint and pressed them on the wall. Then he stood back, hands on hips.

"Are you sure that's what a crocus looks like?" asked Keith.

Lee scratched his head. "I think so."

Lee dipped his hands into the paint
again.

"STOP!" yelled Miss Bennett. "What *do*
you think you're doing, Lee?"

"Painting crocuses, Miss."

Miss Bennett groaned. "Come with me,
Lee. The rest of you, carry on painting
flowers and baby lambs – but do it
properly!"

We carried on painting lambs and
flowers. It took *hours*.

"This is boring," Keith said. "I know!
Let's have a kind of race – see if we can
finish before Miss gets back."

Everyone agreed. We worked really
hard.

Miss Bennett wasn't very pleased.

"What's this?" she asked.

"It's a daffodil," said Jason. "But I'm
not much good at painting flowers."

"And this?"

"That's the sun," said Jason, "but it went wrong."

"And this looks like . . . a tank," said Miss Bennett.

"It was going to be a lamb," said Keith, "but something funny happened to its nose."

"And can someone tell me what the
cowboys and Indians, the pirates and the
Seven Dwarfs and Dracula are doing?"
asked Miss Bennett.

"Err . . . having a picnic, Miss?" said
Melanie.

"I think you'd better all get washed and
changed," said Miss Bennett, "or you'll be
late for lunch."

Mr Perkins, the caretaker, spent all afternoon washing our mural off the playground wall. It took him *hours*.

But next year, we had a new Head Teacher, Mrs Walker.

One morning, at the end of Assembly, she said, "This week is going to be a *special* week. This week we're going to . . ."

Also available in First Young Puffin

BEAR'S BAD MOOD
John Prater

Bear is cross. His father wakes him up much too
early, his favourite breakfast cereal has run out and
his sisters hold a pillow-fight in his room. Even
when his friends, Dog, Fox and Mole arrive, Bear
just doesn't feel like playing. Instead, he runs away
– and a wonderful chase begins!

GOODNIGHT, MONSTER
Carolyn Dinan

One night Dan can't get to sleep. First of all he sees a
strange shadow on the wall. Then he sees huge teeth
glinting and hairy feet under the bed. It couldn't really
be a monster – could it?

RITA THE RESCUER
Hilda Offen

Rita Potter, the youngest of the Potter children, is a
very special person. When a mystery parcel arrives at
her house, Rita finds a Rescuer's outfit inside and races
off to perform some very daring rescues.